Stay bug free!

Susie Brul

The Sick Bug

by Susie Bazil

Illustrated by Shawn McCann

BEAVER'S
POND
PRESS

www.BeaverspondPress.com

www.thesickbug.com

ISBN 10: 1-59298-243-3
ISBN 13: 978-1-59298-243-1

Library of Congress Catalog Number: 2008930355

Printed in the United States of America
Third Printing: 2013

16   15   14   13   6   5   4   3

Cover and interior design by James Monroe Design, LLC.

BEAVER'S
POND
PRESS

Beaver's Pond Press, Inc.
7108 Ohms Lane
Edina, MN 55439-2129
(952) 829-8818
www.beaverspondpress.com

To order, visit www.BeaversPondBooks.com or call 1-800-901-3480.
Reseller discounts available.

For Sam, Jamie, Tess, & Drew
and to Pete—Ibinu

This book belongs to:

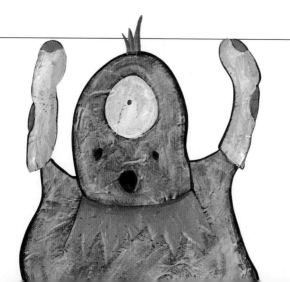

"I don't feel that good, Mommy,"
little Tess said.

"My tummy is hurting
and so is my head."

"Oh dear, you are hot,"
            Mommy said with a sigh.

"You must have a bug!
            Sweet baby, don't cry."

"A BUG! It's a bug?
Where is it? What Kind?"

"It's a sick bug," said Mom.
"They can stay for some time."

"A sick bug is teensy—not easy to find. I know there are more than just one or two kinds."

"Some say they're sparkly
and covered with eyes.

Sticky and prickly with
polka-dot ties."

"Others say silly—fuzzy, furry, and cute.

They giggle and wiggle and wear cowboy boots."

"They put socks on their hands
and gloves on their feet,

but these bugs are strange
creatures you don't want to meet!"

"In fact," Mommy said
        with a far-away look,

"when I was a girl,
        my Mom had a book.

"A book about SICK BUGS, about sneezes and colds.

Sore throats and the sniffles and bad tummy woes."

"So, when will it leave? Will my SICK BUG GO HOME?"

Tess cried with some hope and a sick bug-like moan.

"As I recall from that book long ago,
it's easy to do but takes time, you should know."

"You must drink lots of LIQUIDS and get lots of REST.
Before long he'll be gone. You'll be back to ol' Tess."

"His bug boss will tell him, 'This job can't be done!'

'We can't keep her down; THIS KID'S A TOUGH ONE!'"

"He'll wave his white flag
        while he scurries away.

'She beat me! She beat me!'
        that SICK BUG will say."

"He may even share a good story 'bout YOU!"

"So the lesson to learn, and never forget:

Take care of yourself, and the sick bug will quit."

"You'll drink all your juices; you'll sleep like a champ,

you'll take back the spot where that bug set up camp."

"So Tess, take a sip, close your eyes, get some rest.
Let's show that SICK BUG you are doing your best!"

... and soon you'll be back in the SICK BUG-FREE ZONE!"